THE DINOSAUR THAT POOPED HALLOWEEN!

Tom Fletcher and Dougie Poynter
Illustrated by Garry Parsons

PUFFIN

Danny and Dino had been trick-or-treating,
And now they were full of the sweets
they'd been eating.

They'd eaten a lot,
But they still wanted more . . .

"Come on!" said Danny.
"Let's try one last door!"

A creepy old witch, cackling:

So they ran up the staircase . . .

and hid in the loo.

But the toilet was haunted by . . .

"Run!" Danny cried . . .

and they raced down the halls,

Past spooky old pictures

that hung on the walls.

The witch and the ghosts
were hot on their tail,
And Danny and Dino
were looking quite pale!

Then they spotted a ladder . . .

. . . that led to the attic.

The spooks loomed in from every side.
There was nowhere to run to – and nowhere to hide!

With a feeling of fear in the dinosaur's gut,
Its brain brewed a trick involving its butt.

It knew there was only one thing it could do.
To survive Halloween, it needed to . . .

POO!

Dino pooped candy all over the place.
The vampires and werewolves were
splooshed in the face . . .

The witch and her broomstick
were stuck in the poo.

(The ghosts tried to hide,
jumping back in the loo!)

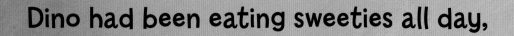

Dino had been eating sweeties all day,

And his colourful poop
helped the friends get away!

Halloween can seem scary –
that much is true . . .

But spooks are less frightening
when covered in . . .

To Alan Grant: They poop in turds . . .
They *do* poop in turds – T.F. & D.P.

For C & K, my little horrors! – G.P.

PUFFIN BOOKS
UK | USA | Canada | Ireland | Australia | India | New Zealand | South Africa
Puffin Books is part of the Penguin Random House group of companies
whose addresses can be found at global.penguinrandomhouse.com.

Penguin
Random House
UK

First published 2022
001
Copyright © Tom Fletcher and Dougie Poynter, 2022
Illustrated by Garry Parsons
The moral right of the authors has been asserted
Printed in China

The authorized representative in the EEA is
Penguin Random House Ireland, Morrison Chambers,
32 Nassau Street, Dublin D02 YH68

A CIP catalogue record for this book is available from the British Library
ISBN: 978–0–241–48883–6

All correspondence to:
Puffin Books, Penguin Random House Children's
One Embassy Gardens, 8 Viaduct Gardens, London SW11 7BW

MIX
Paper from
responsible sources
FSC
www.fsc.org
FSC® C018179